With each descriptive passage, McKnight D'Andrea leads her reader ever deeper into the unspoiled beauty of her treasured blackberry patch. Seasoned berry pickers will recognize each sensory detail while the uninitiated will be tempted to don their protective clothing and head for the brambles in search of the precious fruit. *The Blackberry Patch* is a beautifully written expression of profound gratitude for the gifts of nature and the author's genuine sense of wonder radiates from every page.

Brenda L. Lemon
Library Media Specialist

The Blackberry Patch is an exciting read into the sights, sounds, and smells of blackberry picking. With each descriptive page, McKnight D'Andrea lets readers experience the joys and wonder of the blackberry patch.

Cara Dingus Brook
The Foundation for Appalachian Ohio

Thank you, Lord, for blackberries
For AJ and Tony

Published by Tate Publishing & Enterprises, LLC
127 E. Trade Center Terrace | Mustang, Oklahoma 73064 USA
1.888.361.9473 | www.tatepublishing.com

Tate Publishing is committed to excellence in the publishing industry. The company reflects the philosophy established by the founders, based on Psalm 68:11,
"The Lord gave the word and great was the company of those who published it."

Book design copyright © 2009 by Tate Publishing, LLC. All rights reserved.
Cover and Interior design by Elizabeth A. Mason
Illustration by Benton Rudd

Published in the United States of America
ISBN: 978-1-60696-377-7
1. Juvenile Nonfiction: Science & Nature: Flowers & Plants
2. Juvenile Nonfiction: Sports & Recreation: Camping & Outdoor Activities
09.04.23

The Blackberry Patch

written by

Gina McKnight D'Andrea

TATE PUBLISHING & *Enterprises*

*S*tanding in the humid morning mist in a long-sleeve flannel shirt and overalls with the pants legs tucked into my knee gum boots, I choke at the smell of myself covered with the essential layering of insect repellent like a coat of paint all over my body. No serious blackberry picker would be caught without this protection.

I know my precautions to protect myself from the foliage, fauna, and swarming varmints are not unwarranted. Just ahead of me is the most lush, mosquito-infested blackberry patch you have ever seen!

In the misty air above the leafy patch, mourning doves flutter in their coats of grey, startled by my appearance in their sheltered forest retreat. They coo their sad tune as I approach the blackberry patch.

Walking on the soft, loamy forest floor, I keep an eye out for slithery snakes that thrive in the shady underbrush.

*S*urrounded by the heavy odor of sumac and the sweet smell of honeysuckle, I see the blackberries the size of large gumdrops hanging from the brambly bushes. The morning sun's rays – breaking through the thick array of hickory, buckeye, and sycamore trees – shine a light on the berries that, along with the morning dew, makes them appear as a treasure chest of gems instead of filling for a pie. I know that God has tended this radiant patch just for me.

With my galvanized bucket in hand, bending and reaching, I gently remove each shimmering berry from the bush and place it in my bucket, being careful not to burst the purplish-black beads of juice that make up each fragile berry. The brambles grab my flannel shirt as I probe deep into the brush for the best berries.

Picking my way through the thorny patch, I come upon a small brook that rambles into a glistening waterfall. Around the brook are blue-green dragonflies with net-veined wings resting on logs covered by a luxurious green carpet of moss.

Suddenly, I see a fluffy-tailed red squirrel scurry up the bark of an old hickory tree standing tall and supreme by the brook. Around the old hickory tree are ancient-looking ferns with feathery fronds that give a prehistoric feeling to my blackberry patch.

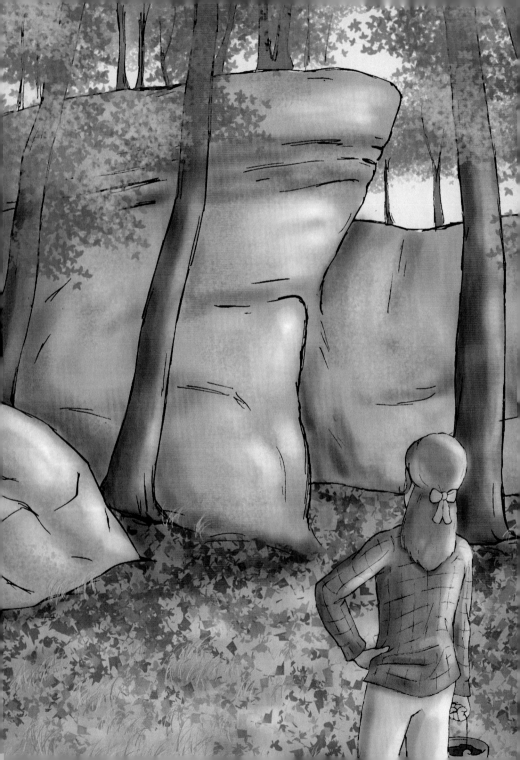

B eyond the brook and the old hickory tree are huge rock cliffs extending from the hillside. The Shawnee Indians lived amongst these cliffs many years ago. Their essence still remains. Maybe they, too, have picked berries from my blackberry patch and enjoyed the savory, robust flavor that melts in my mouth. Only nature could provide such a wonderful morsel.

As I hear a train whistle blow in the distance, I resume my picking, not wanting to realize at this particular moment that civilization is just over the next hill, oblivious to my blackberry patch.

*M*y bucket full, I head for home
dreaming of the delicious treats
I can make with my blackberries.

⊖|LIVE

listen|imagine|view|experience

AUDIO BOOK DOWNLOAD INCLUDED WITH THIS BOOK!

In your hands you hold a complete digital entertainment package. Besides purchasing the paper version of this book, this book includes a free download of the audio version of this book. Simply use the code listed below when visiting our website. Once downloaded to your computer, you can listen to the book through your computer's speakers, burn it to an audio CD or save the file to your portable music device (such as Apple's popular iPod) and listen on the go!

How to get your free audio book digital download:

1. Visit www.tatepublishing.com and click on the e|LIVE logo on the home page.
2. Enter the following coupon code:
   0fd8-8da2-041f-f38e-94c5-361b-dc78-339e
3. Download the audio book from your e|LIVE digital locker and begin enjoying your new digital entertainment package today!